Weekly Reader Books presents

THE HAPPY BIRTHDAY PRESENT

by Joan Heilbroner

Pictures by Mary Chalmers

An I CAN READ Book

Harper & Row, Publishers, New York and Evanston

To Bobby, with love,

and, of course,

To Peter and David

This book is a presentation of Weekly Reader Books.
Weekly Reader Books offers book clubs for children from
preschool through junior high school.

For further information write to:
Weekly Reader Books
1250 Fairwood Ave.
Columbus, Ohio 43216

THE HAPPY BIRTHDAY PRESENT

Text Copyright © 1962 by Joan Heilbroner
Pictures Copyright © 1962 by Mary Chalmers
Printed in the United States of America

Library of Congress catalog card number: 62-12094

THE HAPPY

BIRTHDAY PRESENT

"Davy," said Peter.

"Do you know what day it is?"

"Yes, I do," said Davy.

"It is today."

"No, silly," said Peter.

"It is Mother's birthday."

"We must tell her!" said Davy.

"She knows," said Peter.

"I am going to get a present

for her," said Peter.

"May I come with you?" asked Davy.

"Will you be good?" asked Peter.

"I will," said Davy.

"Come on, then," said Peter.

"Is this where I get my present?"

asked Davy.

"No, Davy," said Peter.

"It is not your birthday.

It is Mother's birthday.

We are going to get

a present for her."

"Oh!" said Davy.

"What do you think

Mother would like?" asked Peter.

"A dump truck," said Davy.

"Mother does not want

a dump truck!" said Peter.

"Roller skates?" asked Davy.

"No," said Peter.

9

"Mother would like a lipstick,"
said Peter.

"Go in and ask the man," said Davy.

10

"You ask him," said Peter.

"O.K.," said Davy. "I will."

11

"I want a lipstick," said Davy.

"What color do you want?"

asked the man.

"We have Red, Real Red, Very Red,

Fire Red, Rose Red or Pink."

"Green," said Davy.

"We have no green lipstick,"

said the man.

"But you may have this lollipop.

It is green."

"Thank you," said Davy.

"Did you get the lipstick?"

asked Peter.

"No," said Davy.

"But the man gave me a lollipop."

"I will ask in the next store,"

said Peter.

14

"What do you sell here?"

asked Peter.

"Hats," said the lady.

15

"Please show me a hat

for a lady," said Peter.

16

"What size?" asked the lady.

"What?" said Peter.

"How big?" asked the lady.

"About down to her ears," said Peter.

"Look at me!" said Davy.

"My!" said the lady.

"Come on, Davy," said Peter.

18

"Look!" said Davy.

"I found a feather!"

"You did not find it," said Peter.

"It came off that hat.

Now, be good."

"I will," said Davy.

19

"Look at all the pretty things!"
said Davy.

"See the things you pin
on your ears," said Peter.

20

"The ones with the stars on them?"

said Davy. "I like them."

"So do I," said Peter.

"We will take them."

21

"That will be five dollars, please,"
said the man.

"Oh, dear!" said Peter.

22

"I forgot about money."

"Davy, do you have any money?"

asked Peter.

"A hundred dollars," said Davy.

"Really?" said Peter.

"A million," said Davy.

"That is silly," said Peter.

"How much do you really have?"

"A penny," said Davy.

"That is not a penny," said Peter.

"That is a dime."

"I am sorry," said Peter.

"We cannot take the earrings.

We cannot pay for them."

"Never mind," said the man.

"Here. Take these paper clips.

They are pretty, too."

"Thank you," said Peter.

"That is all right," said the man.

"But please ask your brother
to come out of my clock."

25

"They might have something here
that Mother could use," said Peter.
"How about that hair brush?"
asked Davy.
"That is not a hair brush!"
said Peter.

"That is a scrubbing brush!"

"That is a nice present," said Davy.

"Mother loves to scrub things,"

said Peter.

"She likes to scrub me," said Davy.

"Let's not go in there!"

"Look, Peter! A zoo!" said Davy.

"That is not a zoo," said Peter.

"That is a pet store."

"Let's get a pet for Mother,"

said Davy.

"Yes!" said Peter.

"Do you have elephants?" asked Davy.

"Not today, little boy," said the man.

"Is that a real sea shell from the sea?"

asked Peter.

"The real thing," said the man.

"How much is it?" asked Peter.

"You can have it," said the man.

"Oh! Thanks!" said Peter.

"Look, Peter! Mice!" said Davy.

"Mother would love a mouse!"

"Is this a present for your mother?"
asked the man.

"Yes," said Peter.

34

"Try the store next door,"

said the man.

"Davy!" said Peter.

"Can you read what that says?"

"Yes, I can," said Davy.

"What?" said Peter.

" 'Keep off the Grass!' " said Davy.

"It says GIFT SHOP," said Peter.

"They may have a present in there."

36

"Is that a gift?" asked Davy.

"Of course," said Peter.

37

"You go in," said Davy.

"I will stay here."

38

"All right," said Peter.

"But stay right on this step!"

"I will," said Davy.

"Pinwheels and balloons!"

sang the man.

"Balloons and pinwheels!"

"How much is that pinwheel?"

asked Davy.

"You can have it for ten cents,"

said the man.

"I only have a dime," said Davy.

"That will do just as well,"

said the man.

"Did you find a present?" asked Davy.

"No," said Peter.

"But the lady gave me this.

It is for flowers, I think."

"I got something, too," said Davy.

"Davy!" said Peter.

"Did you spend your dime?"

"I ate it!" said Davy.

"Did you really eat it?" said Peter.

"No," said Davy.

"I got a pinwheel with it."

"Oh, dear!" said Peter.

"Now we have no present for Mother.

And we have no more money."

48

"I am sorry, Peter," said Davy.

"Never mind," said Peter.

49

"Oh, Davy!" said Peter.

"I have a good idea!

I will tell you about it

on the way home."

"We could give Mother my lollipop,"
said Davy.

"It is almost as big as it was
when I got it."

51

"My goodness, boys! It is late!"

said their mother.

"Where have you been all this time?"

"We went to get you a present,"

said Peter.

53

"A lot of presents!" said Davy.

"For your birthday."

"Oh my!" said their mother.

"I almost forgot it was my birthday!"

"I told you to tell her," said Davy.

55

"Come and see your present,"

said Peter.

"Yes," said Davy, "come and see it."

"How nice!" said their mother.

"Thank you very much!"

"We made it," said Davy.

"Look at all the things!"

"We went to every store in town,"
said Peter.

"The Drug Store, the Hat Store,

the Clock and Earring Store,

the Pet Store and the Gift Shop."

"I see," said their mother.

"But not the Scrubbing Brush Store,"
said Davy.

"Do you really like it?" said Peter.

"It is beautiful," said their mother.

"It is the nicest present I ever had!"

"It is a Christmas tree!" said Davy.

"No, Davy," said Peter.

"I told you.

It is not a Christmas tree."

"What kind of a tree is it," said Davy,
"if it is not a Christmas tree?"

"I think," said their mother,

"that I will call it...

A HAPPY BIRTHDAY TREE!"

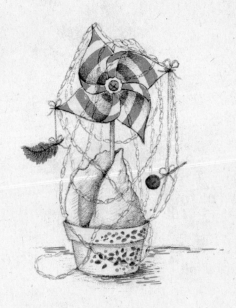